1 2 3 4 5 6 7 8 9 10
❖
First Edition

RAINBOW FISH
PUFFER CRIES SHARK

Text by Sonia Sander

Illustrations by Benrei Huang

 HarperFestival®

A Division of HarperCollins*Publishers*

Rainbow Fish and his friends

love to play tag.

"I bet you can't catch me!"

shouted Puffer.

He jetted into Mrs. Crabbitz's

sculpture garden.

"I bet we can," said Rainbow Fish.
But just as they were about to tag
Puffer, a shadow darkened the edge
of the garden.

Puffer puffed up and yelled, "Shark!"

The shadow moved closer and closer.

Frightened, the little fish scattered.

They all zipped and zoomed

behind Mrs. Crabbitz's sculptures.

Everyone but Puffer.

"Why are you little fish hiding

in my garden?" snapped Mrs. Crabbitz.

"Mrs. Crabbitz!" cried Rainbow Fish.

"We are so glad it is you.

Puffer told us a shark was coming."

"A shark?" asked Mrs. Crabbitz.
"Are you trying to scare your
friends, Puffer?"
She did not think that was
very funny.

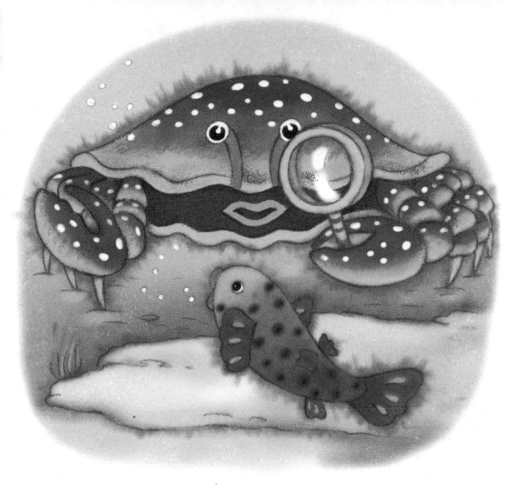

"Oh, no, I . . . I would never do that,"
Puffer stammered.

He told Mrs. Crabbitz that her
shadow looked like that of a shark.

"Hmph," she grumbled.

"That's a likely story."

The next day, the fish played in
the Shallows.

"You'll never catch me!" Puffer called.

Rosie raced to the right.

Spike splashed to the left.

Puffer was cornered.

Once again, he cried, "Shark!"

Rainbow Fish and his friends

looked up.

A huge shadow was moving

toward them!

The fish quickly hid among the coral

and the seaweed.

Everyone but Puffer.

"Old Nemo!" said Angel, relieved, when the giant turtle appeared. "You young fish should really be a little more careful about shouting out 'shark,'" said Old Nemo.

"But . . . but I really thought you were
a shark," said Puffer.

"Then it is odd that you did not hide
with your friends," said Old Nemo.

"Well, I . . . that is, I finally realized
it was you . . . at the last minute,"
said Puffer.

"It sounds a little fishy to me,"
said Spike.

"To me, too," said Rainbow Fish.
The friends told Puffer they
would not fall for his tricks again.

After school, the little fish played
in the Oyster Beds.
"Remember, Puffer, no more
tricks," said Rainbow Fish.

Puffer promised.

"Catch me if you can!" he said.

But as soon as Puffer was surrounded,
he yelled, "Shark! Shark! Shark!"
Just as before, a shadow loomed in
the distance.

"Nice try, Puffer," Spike said.

"I am sure it is just Miss Cuttle."

The fish kept playing.

The shadow moved closer and closer.

"But there really *is* a shark!"
Puffer cried.

"Very funny,"
Rosie said, laughing.

"We are not falling for your
tricks this time," added Dyna.

No one would listen to Puffer.

The shark swam closer.

27

Luckily, Jonah the whale was
nearby patrolling the reef.

He scared the shark away.

Jonah called the young fish

over to the edge of the reef.

"Didn't you see the shark?"

Jonah asked.

"You should have listened to Puffer."

"But we didn't know he was telling

the truth," said Rainbow Fish.

"He has tricked us twice before."

"Well, Puffer, it looks like your tall tales put you and your friends in danger," said Jonah.

"I promise to never, ever, ever make that mistake again," said Puffer.

"Not in a million years!"